This book belongs to ★

....

....

....

Miranda the
Castaway

James Mayhew

Dolphin

for Judith, with thanks

Published as a Dolphin Paperback in 1997
First published in Great Britain in 1996
by Orion Children's Books
a division of the Orion Publishing Group Ltd
Orion House
5 Upper St Martin's Lane
London WC2H 9EA

A catalogue record for this book is available
from the British Library.

Designed by Dalia Hartman
Printed in Italy
ISBN 1 85881 429 4

Miranda was shipwrecked.
She was cast away on a desert
island, all by herself.

She waited to be rescued,
but no one came.

Miranda didn't know what she was supposed to do.

The sharks knew what to do.
Miranda watched them eat fish.
She watched the turtles eat seaweed,
and the birds eat fruit and drink nectar,

and the snakes eat birds,
and the monkeys eat nuts.
She saw that even the spiders
knew what to eat.

Miranda wanted some food and water.

But seawater was too salty.   And the pools were full of insects.

At last she found a spring with clean fresh water and she drank some.

Miranda took the braces
off her teeth, tied them to
a shoelace and caught a fish.
But she couldn't bear to eat
it, and threw it back into
the sea.

Then Miranda wondered if there was any fruit she could eat.

She struggled through the trees and recognised mangoes and starfruit,
bananas and monkey nuts. She ate lots of them.

By now Miranda was tired and wanted to go to sleep. The sharks rested in the water. The turtles laid their eggs on the sand. The birds had their nests, the snakes and spiders their holes. The monkeys had their trees. Miranda tried to sleep on the beach under the stars, but it was cold, and the sounds of the sea and the island kept her awake.

So the next morning, Miranda decided to build a house of her own. She thought she would be safest in a tree. She put logs between the branches for the floor. She gathered leaves and wove them together with creepers to make the walls, and filled the gaps with mud.

She magnified the sun with her glasses and started a fire.
It would keep her warm at night and be useful for cooking.

It was hard work fetching water, so Miranda
hollowed out bamboo sticks to make giant
straws that ran all the way from the spring...

. . . to the treehouse.

Every day Miranda found new
 things to use on the island.
She used shells to eat off.
Coconuts to drink from.

She pulled threads from the
vines to use as string.
She made necklaces with stones
and shells, a sunhat out of leaves.

She planted seeds and grew flowers
and vegetables in her garden.

Miranda built more and more.

She built a bedroom,

a kitchen,

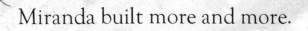

a bathroom,

even a toilet.

Miranda was having fun on the island.
No school, no bedtime, definitely no
bath and hairwash night. It seemed she
had everything she could possibly need.

One day she saw a ship, and she waved and shouted.
But nobody saw her because she was so small.

Miranda waited for the ship to come back. But it never did.

Miranda felt lonely.

The sharks had each other. The turtles had a big family.
So did the monkeys and all the other animals.
Even the spiders had a family.

She tried to make friends with them.
It wasn't the same.

So Miranda built a raft.

Miranda was sad to leave her garden and her treehouse.
But she didn't belong on the island.

It was time to go home.